Lincoln Peirce

BiG NATE
FLIPS OUT

HarperCollins *Children's Books*

For Nate and Al

Also by Lincoln Peirce

Big Nate: The Boy with the Biggest Head in the World

Big Nate Strikes Again

Big Nate on a Roll

Big Nate Goes for Broke

Big Nate: Boredom Buster

Big Nate: Fun Blaster

Big Nate: What Could Possibly Go Wrong?

Big Nate: Here Goes Nothing!

First published in Great Britain by HarperCollins *Children's Books* in 2013
HarperCollins *Children's Books* is a division of HarperCollinsPublishers Ltd,
77–85 Fulham Palace Road, Hammersmith, London, W6 8JB.

www.harpercollins.co.uk

8

Text and Illustrations © 2013 United Feature Syndicate, Inc.

The author asserts the moral right to be identified as the author of this work.

ISBN 978-0-00-747827-9

Printed and bound in England by Clays Ltd, St Ives plc

CHAPTER 1

"You're such a slob."

I turn around. Francis is shaking his head in disgust.

He rolls his eyes. "No, I was talking to the drinking fountain," he says. Then he mutters something about "the messiest kid at P.S. 38."

Just a little background here: P.S. 38 is our middle school. Francis is my best friend. And, yeah, I'm a little messy. So what?

Francis starts to swing his notebook at me, then stops himself. He doesn't want any teachers to catch him clocking me in the head. Around here, assault with a three-ring binder is worth at least a couple of detentions. And Francis never gets detention. EVER.

See? The detention lady doesn't even know his NAME. That says it all.

People think it's weird that Francis and I are so tight, and do you know what? They've got a point. He and I are total opposites. Here's what I mean:

④ HE ACTS LIKE MY AUNT PATTY*

Chew at least **TWENTY TIMES** before swallowing!

And then **FLOSS** after eating!

*He doesn't have a moustache like Aunt Patty, but otherwise the similarities are **UNCANNY!**

Okay, here's an FYI: Francis isn't really this much of a weenie. I think I wrote this study guide back when I was annoyed with him for hanging air fresheners in our tree house. Anyway, read on.

⑤ HE'S AN ONLY CHILD

HIM: spoiled rotten

ME: treated rotten

my sister Ellen

noogie noogie

⑥ HE'S A TOTAL *NEAT FREAK!*

Of **COURSE** I iron my tube socks!

Who **DOESN'T?**

Me and Francis in kindergarten

Maybe the neatness thing should have gone at the TOP of the list. I've known Francis since kindergarten, and he's ALWAYS been Captain Tidypants. Back then, he wouldn't even play in the sandbox without a package of wet wipes.

TSK! LOOK!

THAT POSTER'S NOT STRAIGHT!

DON'T TRASH IT! RECYCLE IT!

Oh, brother. "What's the big deal about a crooked poster?" I ask him.

"It looks sloppy," he answers, frowning. "It detracts from the hallway's overall feng shui."

"Hilarious, Teddy," I grumble, rubbing the bump on my head. "You've still got it. . ."

Great. Science with Mr Galvin. Ever sit through a late-night infomercial for one of those useless kitchen appliances? That's what science is like – except you can't change the channel.

"Nicely done, Gina," Mr Galvin says. She flashes her usual smirk.

"Francis, great job," he says next. I look over, and Francis holds up his paper so I can see it.

An A! No big surprise there. But it's good news just the same, because Francis and I did the homework together. So if HE got an A. . .

Huh? "See me at my desk"? Where's my "nicely done"? Where's my "great job"?

"Uh. . . OK," I say a little nervously. No, a LOT nervously.

"This is, without a doubt," he announces, his voice rising. . .

...THE MESSIEST HOMEWORK ASSIGNMENT I'VE EVER SEEN!

I hear snickering behind me. Nice of him to broadcast that little nugget to the entire class. Couldn't he have chewed me out in PRIVATE?

Whatever. I'm not going down without a fight.

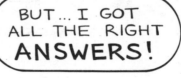

BUT... I GOT ALL THE RIGHT ANSWERS!

"I couldn't even READ your answers!" Mr Galvin goes on. He's in full-blown rant mode now. "Your HANDWRITING is completely ILLEGIBLE!..."

He flips my paper over.

Whoops. Didn't realise I'd started my latest comic masterpiece on the back of my science homework.

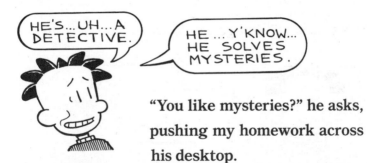

"You like mysteries?" he asks, pushing my homework across his desktop.

Yikes, did THIS ever blow up in my face. Three minutes ago I thought I had an A. Now I'm practically getting expelled.

Mr Galvin's voice follows me as I shuffle back to my seat. "I want that assignment on my desk tomorrow, completely redone."

It's a note from Francis. I sneak a quick peek at Mr Galvin, who's busy showing Mary Ellen Popowski how to light a Bunsen burner without setting her hair on fire. The coast is clear.

HEH HEH!

Yeah, I know: You can't read it. You're not SUPPOSED to. Francis and I spend a lot of time making sure that NOBODY can. What good is having a secret code if half the world knows what it means?

Well. . . all right, just so you can follow along, I'll let you see the key. BUT DON'T SHOW IT TO ANYBODY ELSE!

I write back:

Good ol' Francis.

Finally the bell rings, and we file out. That's the
only thing I like about science: It feels great when
it's over.

". . .Which is exactly why we should go to the
meeting!" Francis says. "Let's make a Chronicle
that's MEMORABLE for a change!"

Yeah. For all the wrong reasons.

MAJOR MISTAKES
IN LAST YEAR'S
"CHRONICLE"

- A bunch of pictures were upside down.

- Next to Chad's name it said: "Most Likely To Be First Woman Elected President."

- The cafetorium ladies were identified as the "Boys Cross-Country Team."

- Practically everybody's name was misspelled. Including...

Frantics Puppy

Tubby Orzits

Nut Weight

- A whole bunch of clubs and teams got completely left out.

IT'S NOT *FAIR!*

Dee Dee, President of the Drama Club

- On the lower right corner of every page there was a really cool picture of a bulldog. There's only one problem: **OUR MASCOT IS A _BOBCAT!_**

- The book was dedicated "To Mrs Godfrey, a great friend and teacher." Uh... **SAYS WHO??**

What a train wreck. There were more mistakes than Chad has freckles. I started to count them, but I got bored when I hit triple digits.

"You know why all that stuff went wrong, don't you?" Francis asks.

"Sure," Teddy and I answer together. . .

Nick Blonsky was the Chronicle editor last year. I could have told you he'd screw up. Anyone who spends that much time with his finger up his nose doesn't exactly inspire confidence.

"Who's gonna be the editor THIS year?" I ask.

"Well, whoever it is," Francis says as we walk into
the meeting. . .

CHAPTER
2

Oh, no. NO!!

"GINA?? SHE'S the editor?" Teddy groans.

"Well, what'd you expect?" whispers Francis. "Gina wants to be in charge of EVERYTHING."

Bingo. That's one reason she's about as popular as a fire drill during recess. Here are a few others:

And now back to the meeting, starring Pushy McBossaround.

"OK, Gina, we hear you," I tell her. "You can lose the stinkin' hammer."

"It's called a GAVEL, genius. . ."

Nice. Now she's THREATENING us. Is this a year-book meeting or a game of Whack-A-Mole?

Gina obviously doesn't care that nobody's paying attention to her, because she launches into some bragfest about taking the Chronicle in a "new direction."

"Sounds good," I tell the guys. "She can go HER way. . ."

"Why not?"

Francis nods towards Gina. "Do we really want the yearbook in HER hands?"

SHE'LL MAKE IT ALL ABOUT **HERSELF!**

Now THAT's bad. You thought a Blonsky-ised Chronicle was scary? A Gina-fied one would be a NIGHTMARE.

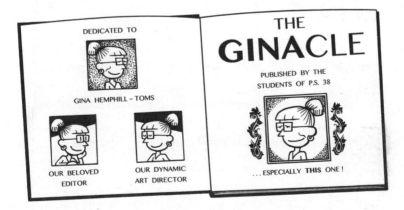

DEDICATED TO

GINA HEMPHILL – TOMS

OUR BELOVED EDITOR

OUR DYNAMIC ART DIRECTOR

THE
GINACLE

PUBLISHED BY THE STUDENTS OF P.S. 38

... ESPECIALLY **THIS** ONE!

"You're right," I say. "We can't just sit here and let Gina make herself the queen of the yearbook."

"So what do we do?" Teddy asks.

"Watch," I whisper. I shoot my hand into the air.

Gina peers at me suspiciously.
"What do YOU want?"

Everyone looks stunned. Especially Francis.
"ME?" he says.

"ExCUSE me," Gina sputters, her cheeks flushing,
"but I'm ALREADY the editor!"

"Oh, is that right? Was there an election?. . ."

Gina's face gets redder. "I VOLUNTEERED, if that's what you mean," she growls. "I volunteered FIRST!"

"And Francis volunteered SECOND," I say. "What's the difference?"

Now she's turning a colour I've never even SEEN before. She points the gavel right between my eyes.

"There can't be TWO editors!" she hisses.

That's Mrs Hickson, the school librarian and year-book adviser. She's also the only person who's ever sent Gina to detention. And now she's shooting down Little Miss Control Freak's master plan to take over the Chronicle! HA!

I'm really starting to like this woman.

Uh-oh. Maybe I spoke too soon.

She holds up a book. "Recognise this?"

Sure. I just borrowed it from the library last week. "Zack Birdwatcher Takes the Cake." It was really good. Zack's this kid who gets a parrot for his birthday, but the parrot disappears. So then. . .

She flips through it. "Perhaps you'd care to explain why there are orange smudges on every single page?"

I... UH... I MIGHT HAVE BEEN EATING SOME CHEEZ DOODLES WHILE I WAS READING IT.

She frowns. "I see. And what about this STAIN on the cover?"

OH. I... ✻ KOFF! ✻... I HAD A LITTLE ROOT BEER ACCIDENT.

HEH HEH!

"And look at THIS!" she goes on.

THE SPINE IS BROKEN...

THE BINDING IS FALLING APART...

...AND THE **COVER** IS **TORN**!

I gulp. It IS pretty beat up. "Uh. . . sometimes stuff gets a little crumpled in my locker."

"A LITTLE CRUMPLED? This looks like it went through a LITTER COMPACTOR," she shouts. Wait, aren't librarians supposed to be QUIET?

Yeah, I know. A couple of months ago I had a total space cadet moment and DREW in a library book. That went over like a poop in a punch bowl.

"Nate," she says, "people are different. Some are neat, and others are messy."

Yes, and some enjoy listening to grown-ups flap

their gums, and others don't. Can we move on?

"But when being messy and careless affects other people or their belongings. . ."

"Problem" sounds so negative. How about "lovable quirk"?

"Lecture's over," she says, giving me one last hairy eyeball. "I'll let you get back to your meeting."

Francis and Teddy are on one of the computers. I pull up a chair.

I start to say "nothing," but who am I kidding? I can't keep secrets from the guys. I give them a recap of my one on one with Ol' Silent but Deadly.

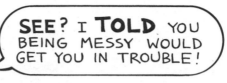

SEE? I **TOLD** YOU BEING MESSY WOULD GET YOU IN TROUBLE!

"No," I remind him. "You told me I was a PIG!"

"A SLOB, not a pig," Francis corrects me.

"Slob. Pig. Let's compromise!" Teddy says. . .

YOU'RE A SLIG!

CLEVER.

WHAT ARE YOU GUYS DOING?

"Alphabetising all the portraits," Francis says. "Some of these are a RIOT!

"Here's Randy!"

"He looks like he's about to throw up."

"You'd throw up, too, if you looked like Randy."

"Lights!. . . Camera!. . . Dee Dee!"

"That smile is so fake."

"Good thing she flossed that day."

"Yikes. Check out the zit on Artur!"

"Wait, IS that a zit?"

"Um, it's either a zit or a small island."

"Let's find YOUR picture, Nate!" Francis grins.

"Let's not," I answer quickly.

Teddy's busting a gut. "Oh, MAN! I'd forgotten how BAD your picture turned out!"

Yeah, because it didn't happen to YOU, that's why. Trust me, I remember it just FINE. It was another episode of. . .

Ta-da. There it is: the lamest picture in the history of the school. Maybe in the history of the UNIVERSE.

"Wow," Teddy gasps, picking himself up off the floor. "And I thought joining the yearbook committee was going to be BORING!"

"Shut up," I grumble.

"Oh, don't take it so seriously, Nate," Francis says.

Yeah, he's right. I just hate looking like such a dweeb. I'd much rather be. . .

CHAPTER 3

"Candids!" I say to Francis and Teddy as we leave
the yearbook meeting.

"It's a picture you take of someone when they don't know you're taking it," Francis explains.

"Now that you mention it," says Francis, rubbing his chin in a co-editor-of-the-yearbook sort of way, "last year's Chronicle had almost NO candids!"

"Yet another reason it stank on ice," Teddy says.

Hey, LOOK, everybody: It's NICK BLONSKY, here to share all his yearbook expertise! No offense, Nick, but isn't that like the captain of the "Titanic" offering to give sailing lessons?

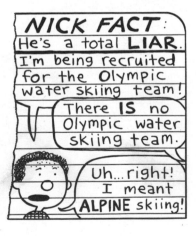

"Oh, it stank, all right," Teddy tells him.

"Those mistakes weren't MY fault," Nick whines.

Ugh. See that? Nick spits when he talks. Every time he says a "P" word, he practically floods the hallway. Anybody got a towel?

Nick snorts so hard, he blows a little snot bubble out of his nose. That's SO nasty.

"Good LUCK!" he sneers. "There's no such thing as a mistake-free yearbook!"

"How nice of him to offer a few words of encouragement," Francis says, rolling his eyes.

"What a dorkus maximus," Teddy grumbles.

"Forget about him, you guys," I tell them.

You're probably thinking: WHAT?? Since when do I go LOOKING for she-who-must-not-be-named? Especially since she's been on a total rampage lately.

YESTERDAY YOU WERE SUPPOSED TO SHARPEN YOUR PENCIL, NOT SPILL SHAVINGS ALL OVER THE FLOOR! SWEEP THAT UP!

"Okay, I'm stumped," Teddy says. "WHY are we going to see Mrs Godfrey?"

"Because she's in charge of the audiovisual room," I explain. "I need to borrow one of the school's cameras. . ."

...SO I CAN START MY CAREER AS **NATE WRIGHT, YEARBOOK PHOTOGRAPHER!**

Francis gives me one of those are-you-crazy? looks.

"Dream ON, Nate! Those cameras are only for TEACHERS!"

"Uh-huh." I nod. "Teachers ANNNNND. . ."

...YEARBOOK EDITORS!

HUH?

"She'll let YOU borrow a camera, Francis!" I point out. "She LIKES you! She REALLY likes you!"

"No, what she LIKES is the fact that I don't do stupid things!" he answers.

...LIKE BRING A CAN OF **SPRAY CHEESE** TO CLASS!

FSSST!

"That may have been a mistake," I admit.

"You're ALWAYS making 'mistakes'!" Francis says, curling his fingers into air quotes. "What if I put myself on the line and borrow the camera. . ."

Teddy chuckles and gives me a shove. "You DO have a way with food!"

Francis is still babbling. "The bottom line is: If you break the camera. . ."

"I'm not going to break it," I object.

". . .or ruin it somehow. . ."

"I'm NOT going to RUIN it!"

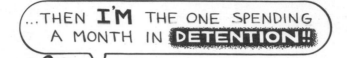

Just the THOUGHT of getting in trouble gives Francis a stress rash. "Listen, that'll NEVER happen," I tell him. "I SWEAR."

I guess I should explain what a "secret swear" is. It's like a pact between me and Francis. Back in third grade we were already best friends, but we wanted to make it official. So we climbed into Francis's tree house and wrote this out:

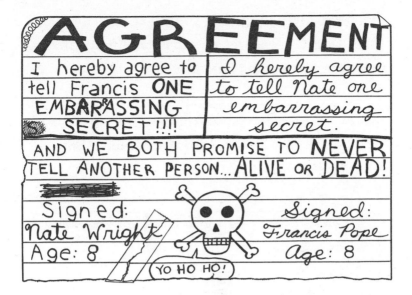

Who knows why we put a skull and crossbones on it. I guess we were in a pirate phase.

Anyway, I told him my biggest secret, and he told me his. And, no, I won't let you know what we said.

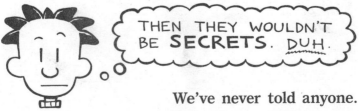

We've never told anyone.

Not even TEDDY. It's a pretty big deal. This sounds kind of cheesy, but it's basically saying that you trust someone with ANYTHING. A secret swear is way more than a promise. It's a stone-cold LOCK.

Francis takes a deep breath. "OK," he says finally. "I'll go ask Mrs Godfrey for the camera. But stay out of sight, Nate."

IF SHE FINDS OUT THE CAMERA'S FOR **YOU**, SHE'LL **NEVER** LET ME BORROW IT!

"He's right," says Teddy matter-of-factly. "Mrs Godfrey hates you."

YEAH, BUT **WHY**?

WHAT DID I EVER DO TO **HER**?

Teddy snickers. "Well. . ."

"Don't answer that," I say quickly.

From around the corner, we hear a door open. Mrs Godfrey's voice comes floating up the hallway.

A few seconds later, here comes Francis – WITH the camera!

"You GOT it!" I exclaim. "Lemme see!"

"Let's wait 'til we get outside," Francis whispers.

We step out into the school yard, and Francis hands over the camera. It's in a leather case, and there's a tag on the strap that says "Property of P.S. 38." How fancy can you get?

"You heard what Mrs Godfrey said, right?" Francis asks. "About it being expensive?"

"Yes. RELAX, will you?" I tell him. "All I'm going to do is take a few pictures!"

Great. It's Randy Betancourt and his band of Merry Morons. As usual, he's acting like a total slimeball.

"Give it back," I growl.

Randy just smirks.

What can we do? If Randy were just one guy, the three of us could take the camera back. But he's NEVER just one guy. And we're no match for his whole posse.

"It's not a PURSE, butthead," Teddy says.

Randy opens his mouth to speak, but then. . .

Coach John walks by.
He hasn't seen us yet. . .
but he MIGHT. Randy nods at his buddies, and they quickly form a wall to block him from Coach John's view. So much for the whole teacher-to-the-rescue thing.

Randy and his posse scatter. I watch in horror as the leather case soars into the sky. In about five seconds, that camera's going to smash into a million pieces on the pavement – unless it doesn't HIT the pavement. I start running.

CHAPTER 4

"Very interesting," Dad says over my shoulder, and I almost jump out of my jammies. Doesn't anybody ever KNOCK around here?

"The part where I'm wearing tights and flying through the air is made up," I tell him.

"Got it." He chuckles, and sits down on the bed. Oh, yippee. Looks like Dad's in one of his tell-me-everything-about-your-life moods.

"Did Randy really get detention?"

I snort. "Are you kidding?"

"And that's coming from an authority on the subject," Dad says. But not in a mean way. He's just busting my chops a little bit.

"So what DID happen?" he asks.

". . .and it wasn't like there was anyplace SOFT for it to land. So I bombed across the school yard. I've never run that fast in my whole LIFE."

"And did you catch it?" Dad asks.

"I was ABOUT to," I grumble. "It was going to be the most amazing catch of all time. Then Kim Cressly got in my way."

YEEP!

"Who's Kim Cressly?"

"Just some girl," I say quickly. No way I'm telling Dad that Kim wants me to be her love puppet. Parents get all weird about that stuff.

"Anyway," I continue, "while I was trying to. . . uh. . . get past Kim, guess who came bumbling along: NICK BLONSKY! And then. . ."

"Let me guess," Dad says. "Nick caught it."

I nod in disgust. "Yes, and believe me, that was a total MIRACLE. He was on my football team last fall. . ."

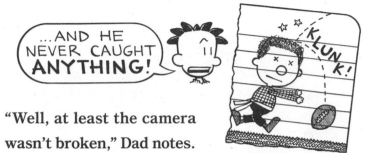

"Well, at least the camera wasn't broken," Dad notes.

"EXACTLY! That's what I told him! But he STILL laid this huge LECTURE on me!"

Dad notices the case next to my bed and opens it.

"Wow," he exclaims. "This IS a nice camera."

"Uh-huh," I agree. "And starting tomorrow, I'll be using it to shoot some KILLER candids!"

"Well, 'Killer,' there's more to being a yearbook photographer than playing Gotcha," he says. "Now go to sleep. It's getting late." He turns to leave.

On the walk to school the next morning, the guys and I talk strategy.

"Chester fell asleep in there last week, and he was drooling all over the beanbag chair!" Teddy laughs.

"Now THAT would have made a great candid!"

"If Chester caught you taking his picture, he'd probably kill you," Francis points out.

"Right," Francis says, rolling his eyes. "I forgot I was talking to a master photographer."

"What was THAT supposed to mean?" I ask the guys. "I haven't even TAKEN any pictures yet!"

Teddy points at the bulletin board. "Uh. . . I think they were talking about THAT one."

"That – that's ME!" I sputter.

"Brilliant observation," Francis deadpans.

Gina. I should have known.

"You think you're funny, Gina?" I snap.

"The 'big idea' was to let people know about Retake Day, genius," she says.

"How, by plastering my picture all over the school?"

"Oh, RELAX," she huffs. "You're on ONE POSTER."

She pulls some sheets from under her arm. "I used plenty of OTHER pictures, too. Look."

"See?" she says with an innocent little grin. "A whole BUNCH of us made posters!"

"That's DIFFERENT! You used my REAL school portrait! THOSE are FAKE!" I shout. "You were trying to look dorky ON PURPOSE!"

"Yes." She smirks. . .

Behind me, Teddy snickers. Remind me to noogie him later.

"Take it down if you want." Gina shrugs. "But if you're so INSECURE that you can't poke fun at yourself. . ."

"I can poke fun at myself just fine," I mutter. "I just don't like when SHE does the poking."

"So what are you gonna do?" Teddy asks.

I open my backpack and pull out the camera. "I have an idea. It's still a little fuzzy. . ."

"Skippy has $20. He buys four bags of tortilla chips to bring to Pepper's party. Each bag costs $2.60. Sales tax is 5 per cent. How much money does Skippy have left?"

I hate problems like this. Plus, what's up with these stupid NAMES? "Pepper" sounds more like a HORSE than a person. And the only Skippy I've ever known was that labradoodle that used to poop every day in Francis's mum's garden.

UHNFFF!... EEEYYUNNNGG...

Uh-oh. I feel a yawn coming on. And that's never a good idea during maths.

First, Mr Staples gets a little squirrelly if you look even a tiny bit bored.

Oh, was I not being *INTERESTING* enough for you? My **APOLOGIES!**

And second, your best friend might almost KILL

you by choosing exactly the wrong moment to
toss you a note.

"Nate!" Mr Staples jumps up from his desk. "Are
you all right?"

I quickly spit out the note and stuff it into my
pocket. "Yeah, I'm OK," I tell him.

"Why don't you go drink some water," he suggests.

Not a bad idea. I'll get a two-minute break from Skippy and Pepper, AND I'll get to read this note that I halfway choked on.

I step into the hallway and fish the note from my pocket. It's a little moist. But readable.

Hmmph. Not so hot, that's how. My target isn't cooperating.

"O.C." stands for Operation Candid. It's my plan to get even with Gina for that little stunt she pulled. She wants to put a goofy-looking picture of me on a poster? Fine.

There's just one minor problem: I don't HAVE a goofy-looking picture of Gina. And I can't seem to GET one, either, because. . . well, this will explain why.

See what I mean? Gina just doesn't do goofy things. I always knew she was obnoxious. But until now, I didn't realise how BORING she is.

Hey, now THAT'S friendly. I come right back at him. "What are YOU doing here?"

He puffs out his chest.

Sounds about right. Hall monitors are dorks.

"You're SUPPOSED to be in class." A spray of Nick spit flies everywhere. "I could REPORT you."

I brush past him and stalk back into the maths room, slamming the door behind me. Whoops. That was kind of loud.

"If you're feeling better, Nate, please resume your work," Mr Staples says.

"What's the matter?" Teddy whispers as I flop back into my seat. "Your EARS!"

NATE FACT:
My ears turn bright red when I get mad.

I roll my eyes and wave him off. There's no need to tell him what a weasel Nick is. He already knows. EVERYBODY does.

I slog through the rest of maths – in case you were wondering, Skippy has exactly $9.08 left – and then, just as the bell rings at the end of the lesson, things start looking up for Operation Candid.

"Did you hear that, guys?" I exclaim as we file out of class. "Here's my big chance!"

Teddy looks confused. "To jump rope?"

"She's about as graceful as a rock in a blender!" I continue. "I bet I can get some GREAT shots of her looking like a total DOOFUS!"

"What's the matter?" Francis asks.

"Nothing, nothing," I answer, my throat tightening. "It's just that. . ."

"The CAMERA?" Teddy says in disbelief.

BUT I SAW YOU WITH IT DURING LUNCH!

"It's here somewhere," I assure him as my heart starts pounding through my chest. But it's NOT here somewhere. With my palms turning sweaty, I paw through the pile again. And again. I'm in full panic mode now.

Then I hear Francis behind me.

I KNEW IT.

"What?" I ask. My voice sounds faraway.

"You lost the camera," Francis says.

"No, I didn't, I just—"

He nods his head. "Yes, you did, Nate. Just admit it. You lost the camera. . ."

...BECAUSE YOU'RE SO MESSY!

"I DID NOT lose it!" I protest. "I'm. . ."

"Oh? Then WHERE IS IT?" he snaps.

"I. . . it's. . ." I stammer.

"You can't answer!" Francis says, his voice rising. "You have NO IDEA where it is!"

YOU PROMISED ME YOU'D BE **CAREFUL** WITH IT, NATE! YOU **SWORE!**

I can feel my ears starting to burn. Francis isn't being fair. It's not like I left the camera lying on the GROUND somewhere. It was in my locker. I KNOW it was!

FRANCIS. CALM DOWN. I **WAS** CAREFUL. I...

"No, you WEREN'T!" Francis explodes. "This is so TYPICAL, Nate! You always screw up, and then I'M the one who has to FIX everything!"

Now I'm mad. "Well, we can't all be PERFECT like YOU, can we?" I say bitterly.

"I never SAID I was perfect!" he yells.

...BUT AT LEAST I'M NOT YOU! AT LEAST I'M NOT A **LOSER**!!

It's like getting punched in the face. Francis has called me a loser before. But not like this. Not like he really MEANS it. I can feel my answer rising in my throat. Before I even know what I'm saying, before I can stop myself, I open my big, fat mouth.

Silence. For the first time, I notice the crowd. Half the school's been listening. And they just heard me break the promise I made to Francis in third grade.

I told them his secret.

A few people laugh along with Randy. Other kids seem stunned. Francis looks pale. He opens his mouth for a second, then closes it. He shakes his head. Then he turns away.

I catch up to him. He doesn't stop walking.

"H-hey," I stutter.

"I shouldn't have. . . I didn't. . ." My voice trails off. I can barely talk.

I start again. "Francis," I say, forcing the words out. "I. . . I made a mistake."

He doesn't even look at me. "So did I," he says.

CHAPTER 6

Yeah, that IS it! Why didn't I think of it BEFORE?

Dee Dee flops down next to me.

"I just figured out who stole that camera from my locker!" I tell her.

Then Dee Dee starts nodding like a dashboard bobblehead. "It sounds like the sort of mondo jerko thing he'd do. . .

. . .But how can you prove it?"

"I'm not sure," I admit. "Maybe just by following him around. Spying on him."

I'm about to tell Dee Dee that the whole point of being a spy is NOT to be noticed, when. . .

We walk in silence – which NEVER happens when Dee Dee's around – but after a few minutes, she can't resist saying something.

Just hearing Francis's name makes my stomach hurt. I don't really want to go there, but Dee Dee's going to keep asking until I spill my guts. So why not? Maybe I'll feel better.

Dee Dee waggles her finger at me. "Never say never, Nate! Sure, Francis is upset NOW. . ."

"Except it's about more than just the camera," I remind her.

"Yes, I know, the whole 'Butthurst' thing," Dee Dee says, waving her hand impatiently.

"Like what?"

"Like mine," she answers. "It's Dorcas."

I snicker. "Sorry. I'm picturing a gazelle named Dorcas."

Good ol' Teddy. At least HE's not mad at me.

He claps his hands once, then rubs them together.
"So!" he says. "What are we gonna do?"

"About what?" I ask.

"About YOU AND FRANCIS, fool!" he answers.

I hadn't really thought of that. It's probably no fun
for Teddy to be stuck in the middle.

Teddy nods. "Just a couple of minutes ago. He was on his way to tell Mrs Godfrey about the camera."

There's no mistaking Mrs Godfrey's voice. It sounds like a head-on collision between a foghorn and a chain saw. Teddy, Dee Dee, and I sneak down the hall towards her classroom to listen in.

Francis isn't easy to hear. "I. . . um. . . can't remember. I must have. . . misplaced it."

There's a pause, then Mrs Godfrey's voice booms again. "This doesn't sound like you, Francis. Are you sure YOU lost the camera?. . ."

I brace myself. Here it comes. Here's where Francis tells her the whole story.

"He didn't rat you out!" Teddy whispers. "What a PAL!"

"Yeah," I mumble, feeling worse than ever.

Mrs Godfrey gives a long sigh. I can practically smell her onion breath from here.

I wince. Hearing that from a teacher will cut Francis to the bone.

"You have detention for one week," Mrs Godfrey continues. "And if the camera doesn't turn up

during that time, you will pay the school the cost
of replacing it."

"Yes, ma'am," Francis says quietly.

"You may go," she tells him.

"Guess he's still mad at you," Teddy says sadly.

"Poor Francis!" Dee Dee cries.

"I'm going to do more than that," I mutter.

Teddy looks baffled. "What do you mean?"

"Francis said it yesterday: I always screw up, and then he has to fix everything."

"People can't just change by snapping their fingers," Teddy scoffs.

Dee Dee's face lights up like a Christmas tree. "Not unless they're HYPNOTISED!"

All three of us speak at once.

UNCLE PEDRO!

Teddy's Uncle Pedro is. . . well, it's hard to describe him. He's sort of an inventor-magician-handyman-mad scientist sort of guy.

Oh, yeah. And he hypnotises people.

No, I've never been hypnotised. But with the camera missing in action and Francis giving me the silent treatment, it might be my only hope. When school ends, the three of us make a beeline for Uncle Pedro's house.

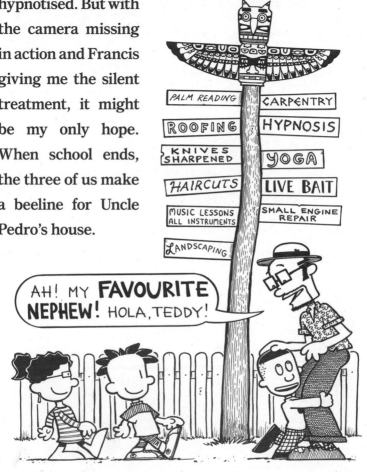

PALM READING CARPENTRY
ROOFING HYPNOSIS
KNIVES SHARPENED YOGA
HAIRCUTS LIVE BAIT
MUSIC LESSONS ALL INSTRUMENTS SMALL ENGINE REPAIR
LANDSCAPING

AH! MY **FAVOURITE NEPHEW!** HOLA, TEDDY!

"Uncle Pedro," Teddy says, "you remember my friends Nate and Dee Dee."

"Absolutely," he says, shaking our hands. He peers at me through his Coke-bottle glasses.

"Yeah, you're RIGHT!" I exclaim. "How'd you know that?"

"Lucky guess," he says simply. "Come inside."

"I was. . . uh. . . wondering if you could make me neater," I say after we sit down.

So I tell Uncle Pedro all about Francis and the camera and everything. Then I wait for him to put some crazy hypno-whammy on me. But he just reaches behind his back, winks at me, and says. . .

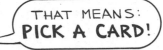

Huh? Is he serious? How's a CARD TRICK going to help?

"Any card," he says, nodding at me.

I don't get it. I was expecting him to wave a watch in my face or something. But I guess I've got nothing to lose. I slide a card from the deck and place it face down on the table.

"Interesting," Uncle Pedro says. "Flip it over again."

I turn the card face down.

"Your card was the seven of spades, correct?"

"Uh-huh," I answer.

WHAT THE...?!

"Hey, how'd you do that??" I ask in astonishment.
"How'd you change it?"

"Me? YOU'RE the one who flipped the card over."

WELL, **I** DIDN'T TURN IT INTO THE JACK OF HEARTS !

Uncle Pedro shrugs.
"Then perhaps there
is no explanation,"
he says.

Okay, I get it. It's a card trick. You're not SUPPOSED
to know how it works. Let's move on.

"Can we start now?" I ask Uncle Pedro.

He shoots me a quizzical look. "Start what?"

"Well," I say, a little confused. "Aren't you going to hypnotise me?"

Uncle Pedro smiles.

CHAPTER 7

"What a rip-off!" I grumble as we leave Uncle Pedro's.

"You don't feel any different?" Dee Dee asks.

"Not a bit," I snort.

Teddy frowns. "Since when are you afraid of a PUDDLE?"

"I'm not AFRAID of it, doofus," I answer.

"Are you CRAZY, Dee Dee?" I shout angrily. "YOU JUST RUINED MY SHIRT!"

"No, I just PROVED A POINT!" she says, grinning like the village idiot.

"NEAT? Open your EYES! I'm a MESS, thanks to you and your little MUD BALL attack!" I growl.

"You never cared about clean clothes BEFORE!" Teddy exclaims. "I think Dee Dee's right! You're HYPNOTISED!"

"We need to make sure of it!" Dee Dee announces. "Let's do another test!"

"No more mud balls," I say quickly.

Mr McTeague is a total whack job about his lawn. No, wait. He's a total whack job, FULL STOP. What else do you call a guy who digs crabgrass out of his yard with a pair of eyebrow tweezers?

Teddy sweeps his arm across the bright green grass. "It's PERFECT, don't you think?"

WELL... NOT **EXACTLY**.

Maybe I just never looked at Mr McTeague's lawn all that carefully before. But I am now. And it's definitely got issues.

THE GRASS AROUND THAT TREE TRUNK ISN'T EVENLY TRIMMED.

THAT SPOT IN THE CORNER IS A DARKER SHADE OF GREEN THAN THE REST OF THE LAWN.

THOSE ACORNS OVER THERE LOOK SORT OF RANDOM.

"Did you really just say the ACORNS are too messy?" Teddy asks in disbelief.

"I'm just pointing out they could be a bit more organised," I explain.

Dee Dee's hopping up and down like a frog on a pogo stick. "EUREKA! That PROVES it!!"

"Wow," I say as Dee Dee goes skipping away. "SOMEBODY'S pretty fired up about this."

"Well, aren't YOU?" Teddy asks.

And speaking of underwear, I've been wearing the same pair of tighty-whities since this morning. That's gross.

Dad's burning something on the stove when I walk through the kitchen door. "Hi, Nate! Want a snack? Supper won't be ready for a while."

"No, thanks. I've got some work to do in my room."

A couple of hours later, Dad knocks on my door.

Dad's lips start moving, but no sound comes out. Either he doesn't know what to say, or he just won a scholarship to mime school.

"Y-you cleaned your room," he finally stammers.

Brilliant observation, Dad. "Yeah," I tell him.

"With my hands. Because it was messy," I explain. Gotta love these father-son chats. They're so DEEP.

Downstairs at the supper table, Ellen continues the sparkling conversation.

"Besides an annoying big sister, you mean?" I ask.

"You've got your napkin in your lap for once,"

she says. "You haven't spilled anything yet. And you're actually CHEWING your food. . ."

" . . .a concept you're obviously too BRAIN-DEAD to understand!"

"You know what I think?" Dad announces in that fake-happy voice he uses whenever he's trying to keep Ellen and me from killing each other.

"No, thanks," I say as I put my dishes in the sink and head upstairs.

Later, Dad pokes his head in my room again.

"I don't," I tell him. "I'm just rewriting my class notes for social studies."

He sits down on my bed, which totally messes up

the blanket. But whatever. I'll fix it later.

"So this isn't something Mrs Godfrey TOLD you to do?" he asks, as one of his eyebrows heads north.

"No, I just wanted to make them neater."

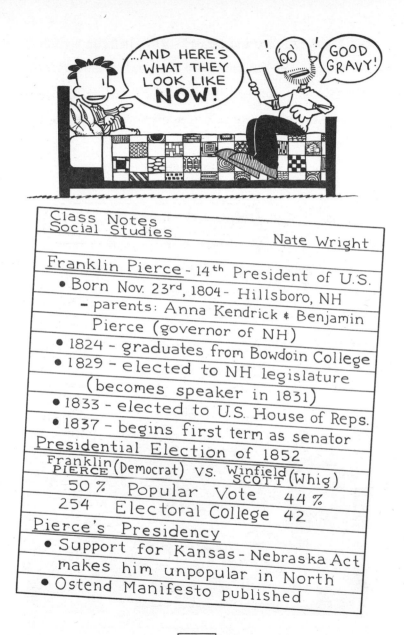

Dad hands me back my notes. He's got the weirdest expression on his face. It's like half worried, half gassy.

Hmm. OK, here's where things get kind of dicey. I'm pretty sure Dad wouldn't be too happy about me getting hypnotised, so I can't tell him why I've turned into Joe Tidy. And if he finds out a camera disappeared from my locker, he's going to call the school. You never want a parent to call the school.

So I lie.

Dad gives me The Squint. He probably knows there's more to the story. But what can he do? Ground me for being too neat?

WELL...
ALL RIGHT,
THEN.

WHY DON'T
YOU GO TO
SLEEP, NATE.
IT'S GETTING
LATE.

"Can I stay up and draw comics for a while?" I ask.

...SORT OF AS A REWARD
FOR CLEANING MY ROOM
WITHOUT BEING ASKED?

He smiles. "I suppose a miracle like that buys you some drawing time. But only half an hour, Nate. It's a school night."

"Thanks, Dad," I tell him. Then I jump into a

brand-new Luke Warm, Private Eye adventure.
I'm just getting started when. . .

"What? You said I had half an hour!"

Dad taps his watch. "That WAS half an hour."

"But I haven't even started DRAWING yet! I barely
finished measuring all the panels!"

I flail around for a good answer. "I just. . . I wanted all the panels to look nice and straight," I say weakly.

Dad peers down at my notebook. "Well, they certainly are nice and straight," he says.

CHAPTER 8

The sun's barely up when I leave for school the next morning. I need to get there early. . .

He doesn't LOOK very sorry, if you ask me. But I'm
so happy to see Francis, I don't even mind getting
clocked in the face by. . . the "Daily Courier"?

FRANCIS! HOW COME
YOU'RE DELIVERING
NEWSPAPERS?

He doesn't look at me. He
won't even slow down. "I
need the money," he says.

A hot wave of guilt washes over me – even though I have nothing to feel guilty about. . .

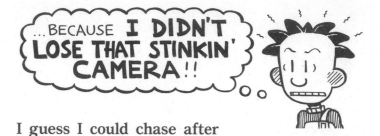

...BECAUSE **I DIDN'T LOSE THAT STINKIN' CAMERA!!**

I guess I could chase after Francis and tell him that. AGAIN. Or I could tell him that he doesn't need to buy the school a new camera, that I'LL pay for it if I have to.

...EXCEPT I **WON'T** HAVE TO!

...ONCE I PROVE THAT **RANDY** TOOK IT!

THEN MAYBE FRANCIS AND I CAN BE **FRIENDS** AGAIN!

The school's pretty empty when I get there. And you know what? It looks GOOD this early.

Mrs Hickson eyes me suspiciously – which makes sense, I guess. I'm usually here an hour AFTER school, not an hour before, if you get my drift.

"I want to clean my locker before home room," I answer.

Hickey looks like she might kiss me. (She doesn't. Phew.) "My goodness, Nate, this is WONDERFUL!" she gushes. "I assumed you'd LOST all these!"

"Nope!" I tell her. "I never lose stuff!. . ."

Or at least, I never USED to. But now that I've been hypnotised, I'm ready to send most of what's in my locker straight to Dump City.

It takes me almost forty-five minutes. What a disgusting job. You wouldn't believe all the stuff that comes out of there.

LOCKER INVENTORY
(not a complete list)

- 13 pairs of unwashed socks
- 3 moulded (and mouldy) plastic mouthguards
- 27 pencils
- 2 unfinished Dr Cesspool comix

BZZZ

- 49 jelly beans
- ½ roll toilet paper
- 2 wooden drumsticks
- 2 chicken drumsticks

Hey! Those are MINE!

- 12.3 pounds of maths homework
- 1 volleyball (deflated)
- 1 pair of Mr Galvin's dentures

mmph!

- 16 empty cheez doodle bags
- 1 sombrero
- the head of a lawn gnome

Ouch!

- 6⅓ cups of dirt

And I won't even get into how it SMELLED. Francis was right. I WAS a slob.

"I'm a SPY!" Dee Dee says, like it's supposed to be obvious. "That's how we TALK!"

"Where, at a BIRD SANCTUARY?" I say.

"No, silly!" She giggles.

"Here's a suggestion, 007," I whisper. "Don't announce to the world who you're about to spy on."

"Got it," Dee Dee says a little sheepishly.

Right. I'll believe it when I see it. Dee Dee's about as low-key as a match in a fireworks factory.

"Oh, and don't forget!" she calls over her shoulder.

My heart sinks. Oh, yeah. The Trivia Slam.

I guess I should fill you in. The Trivia Slam is like the ultimate quiz show. The questions can be about ANYTHING, and the last team standing wins. It happens every year, and it's HUGE.

I'm supposed to be on Francis's team – the
Factoids – along with Teddy, Dee Dee, and Chad.
Talk about a trivia powerhouse. As soon as we put
that group together, we knew we had the goods to
knock off the defending champs. . .

But everything's changed
now. How can I be on the
team. . .

When the bell rings for social studies, I'm
still thinking about the Trivia Slam – until
Mrs Godfrey gets everyone's attention.

Translation: Get ready for Mrs Godfrey to throw a conniption fit if she thinks your notebook is too sloppy. Or too unorganised. Or too red. On a normal day, a notebook check – for me, anyway – is a one-way ticket to detention.

But today's not a normal day.

Mrs Godfrey's eyes look ready to pop out of their sockets as she flips through my notebook, staring at page after perfect page.

Five minutes with Uncle Pedro, that's what. But I just shrug my shoulders. "I decided I wanted to be neater, that's all," I say. Honest enough.

An A DOUBLE plus?? Holy COW!!

Isn't she charming? And so FRIENDLY, too. "There's no mystery, Gina: I've cleaned up my act."

This is killing her.

"Does it LOOK like I'm faking?" I ask. "Get used to the new me, Gina. Neatness is now my way of life."

HA! That's me one, Gina zero. And you want to know the best part? The rest of the day goes EXACTLY THE SAME WAY!

In English, Ms Clarke gives me extra credit for my "phenomenal" penmanship. In maths, Mr Staples tells everybody my homework is the "Mona Lisa of bar graphs."

Even Old Fossil Face is impressed.

Not too shabby, right? As I head for my locker after class, I realise something: I didn't get yelled at today. Not even ONCE. Who knew it was this easy to make teachers happy?

Looks like Dee Dee's still in not-so-secret agent mode. "What's up?" I ask as I turn the corner.

"The pigeon has almost landed!" she whispers.

Not THIS again. "Try it in English, Dee Dee," I tell her. "I can't speak Spy."

"That DOES sound kind of suspicious," I admit, amazed that Dee Dee actually turned up some useful information.

"I'll continue my investigation tomorrow," she says.

I'VE GOT ANOTHER **FABULOUS** OUTFIT PLANNED!

That's good. The "bride of Dracula" look might not work two days in a row.

NOW C'MON, NATE! LET'S NOT KEEP OUR FELLOW FACTOIDS WAITING!

My stomach drops off a cliff. "You know what? I'm going to skip the Trivia Slam, Dee Dee. You guys will do fine without me."

...AND FRANCIS DOESN'T WANT ME THERE, ANYWAY.

"SURE, he does!" Dee Dee chirps a little too quickly.

"Oh, yeah?" I mutter. "Did you ask him?"

She gets a little fidgety. "I. . . I've talked to him about it a couple of times, yes," she answers.

"Well? What did he say? In his EXACT WORDS."

"Uh. . ." Dee Dee mumbles nervously. "He said that. . . that he didn't care if you came or not."

JUST WHAT I THOUGHT. SEE YA.

NATE, WAIT!

"Francis didn't say you COULDN'T come! He just said that. . . um. . ."

I swallow the lump in my throat and start home.

They really WILL do fine without me. The Factoids, I mean. They can beat anybody, as long as they've got Francis. He's always been a trivia geek.

I come to the edge of the Little Woods. If I go to the left and stay on the sidewalk, I'll be home

in ten minutes. But if I go to the right, there's a
shortcut through the woods that leads straight to
my street. It's a little muddy sometimes, but it's
fast.

I go to the left.

CHAPTER 9

I'm starting to hate being neat.

Everything takes so LONG. Like right now, for example. I'm getting ready for school picture Retake Day. . .

Pretty ridiculous, right? NOBODY spends that long on his hair.

But I can't help it. Whatever Uncle Pedro did when he hypnotised me is working TOO well.

Sure, there are some upsides to being a neatnik. Like my GRADES. All of a sudden, I'm getting A's in EVERYTHING.

Plus, I'm not spending my afternoons in detention. I haven't seen Mrs Czerwicki for a WEEK.

IF THIS KEEPS UP, THE OLD GAL WILL BE ABLE TO **RETIRE!**

But look, I didn't get hypnotised to be Joe Honour Roll. I did it to patch things up with Francis. Which isn't working out so hot.

And that's not all. Turning into Mr Clean is ruining all my hobbies. I can't play soccer with the guys because – don't laugh – I'm worried about getting grass stains on my trousers.

HOW LAME IS **THAT?**

Oh, and want to read the latest edition of "Luke Warm, Private Eye"? Well, you CAN'T. I ripped it into a zillion pieces. . .

Huh? What does HE want? I'm used to Principal Nichols looking for me, but not with a SMILE on his face. It's a little creepy.

OK, now it's a LOT creepy. Remember who ELSE is

a hall monitor? Nick Blonsky. Need I say more?

"Oh, I DISAGREE, Nate!" he continues. "Thanks to the recent change in your behaviour. . ."

A BADGE? Why not just stamp "LOSER" on my forehead? It's pretty much the same thing.

"What do you mean?" I ask.

Teddy chuckles and tugs on my tie.

He'll WRINKLE it? LISTEN to me. I sound like a
complete dorkwagon.

"Just don't TOUCH it," Teddy warns Dee Dee. "You
might ruin Nate's swanky OUTFIT!"

"I never said that," I snap.

"You might as well have," Teddy growls.

Dee Dee jumps in. "Guys, GUYS!"

"That's just what I saw the other day!" Dee Dee whispers excitedly. "Randy's showing off the

CAMERA he stole from your locker, Nate!"

Teddy frowns. "How do you know?"

She shakes her head. "I don't, exactly."

"What's she talking about?" Teddy whispers.

I shrug. "Who knows? I try not to spend any time inside Dee Dee's head."

"Good point." Teddy snickers. "That's a weird neighbourhood."

We watch as Dee Dee strolls casually over to Randy and his posse. Then. . .

She hits the floor like a sack of potatoes. Randy drops something. But it's not the camera.

I hear him angrily whisper to his friends as he stoops to the floor.

"Pick WHAT up? What ARE those?" Teddy asks.

"Beats me," I answer as Dee Dee climbs shakily to her feet.

"Well, go faint somewhere ELSE," Randy snarls.

Dee Dee wobbles away from Randy and his gang like a leaky balloon, then finds Teddy and me around the corner.

"What HAPPENED over there?" we both ask.

It's a Gag Me card. Those aren't allowed at P.S. 38. If you get busted with them, you're in big trouble.

"Well, that explains why Randy looked like he was hiding something," Teddy says.

I nod sadly. "Yeah. But it wasn't the camera."

"I'm beginning to think Randy's too STUPID to steal a camera." Dee Dee frowns. "Maybe someone ELSE took it."

Teddy heaves a sigh. "Maybe. But WHO?"

The bell rings. Time for home room.

"Let's talk more about it later, during our free lesson," Dee Dee suggests.

I shake my head. "It'll have to wait 'til lunch."

Which turns out to be as exciting as Mr Galvin's rock collection. All you do is walk up and down the corridors. I feel like those old people who do laps around the mall.

It's Nick. But for a second, I almost don't recognise him. He's walking really fast, and he's all hunched over. I take another look, and. . . HEY!!

Or does he? He's too far away for me to tell for sure. But he's got SOMETHING tucked under his arm. And it sure LOOKS like the camera.

I take off after him.

You're not supposed to run in the hallways – ESPECIALLY if you're a hall monitor. But this is an emergency. I kick it into overdrive and round the corner. Then. . .

What idiot put a DESK here? I scramble off the
floor, ready to crank up my Nick chase again.

He's already way ahead of me.
I can't waste another second.

Then I look around.

The old me wouldn't have worried about a few papers on the floor. I would have sprinted after Nick like a crazed bloodhound. If I'm going to get that stupid camera back, that's what I should do.

But I can't.

I start picking up all the sheets and stacking them on the desk. Not because I want to. Because I HAVE to. Being hypnotised leaves me no choice.

The lunch bell rings. The hallway fills up with people. Whatever chance I had to catch Nick red-handed is long gone.

What a mess.

CHAPTER

10

"I just had a chance to solve the camera mystery, and I BLEW it. . ."

I tell Teddy and Dee Dee about seeing Nick with the camera and how he got away.

Teddy rolls his eyes. "Funny how you never mentioned that, Sherlock."

"I can't take this any more," I say miserably.

"Sorry, dude." Teddy shakes his head. "Uncle Pedro's visiting my grandparents in Mexico. He'll be back in a week."

"I've heard that sometimes a DRAMATIC EVENT can snap a person out of a hypnotic trance!"

"What kind of dramatic event?"

Dee Dee sighs. "I don't know."

OK, NOW we're talking. Cheez Doodles make everything better. And I'm STARVING. I didn't eat breakfast this morning because I was obsessing about my hair, remember? I reach into the bag.

"What's the matter?" Teddy asks.

"I got orange powder all over my hands."

He makes a tell-me-something-I-didn't-know face. "Well, DUH!"

"And so MESSY," I say, pushing the bag away.

THANKS, BUT...
NO, THANKS.

SCOOT!

Teddy's jaw drops.

Dee Dee gasps.

NATE! YOU **LOVE** CHEEZ DOODLES!
YOU WRITE **POEMS** ABOUT THEM!

I know. And now they DISGUST me. I lay my head on the table (after wiping it off with Teddy's napkin) and try to pull myself together. Francis hates me. None of my hobbies are fun any more. And I can't even eat my favourite food in the whole world.

WHAT **ELSE** COULD GO WRONG?

HAW! HEY! **BUTT HURTS!**

HA HA HA HA ! HA

I look across the cafetorium, and I feel like throwing up. This is my fault. I spilled the beans about Francis's middle name. I might as well have painted a bull's-eye on his back.

The blood starts pounding in my head. The lunchtime noises fade away, until all I can hear is Randy's voice and his stupid laugh as he aims another kick at Francis's butt. I stand up.

Then I flip out.

OK, true confessions time: I've never been in a real fight before. So jumping on Randy like a rabid wolverine might not have been one of my better ideas. But it goes pretty well at first. In fact, I might actually be WINNING when. . .

"He ATTACKED me!" Randy whimpers, switching to victim mode in a millisecond.

Mrs Czerwicki nods grimly. "I saw it."

"Not ALL of it," comes a familiar voice.

Mrs C. looks surprised. "This really doesn't concern you, um. . . er. . ."

"Francis," he says helpfully.

"Yes, well, thank you for your input, Francis. . ."

Great. Nothing like a little quality time with the Big Guy. I won't bore you with the details. Basically, he yells at me. Nonstop. For about half an hour.

"Hey," says Francis.

"Oh. Uh. . . hey," I answer, trying to sound casual.

He nods towards the principal's office. "What did he say?"

"Just what I KNEW he'd say," I snort.

THAT I SHOULDN'T HAVE **PICKED ON** POOR, INNOCENT **RANDY!**

Francis shakes his head. "That's so bogus."

I shrug. "I guess I DID sort of ambush him. But he deserved it."

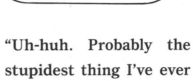

SO... UH... ANYWAY... YOU GOT HYPNO-TISED, RIGHT?

"Uh-huh. Probably the stupidest thing I've ever done."

"Why? I mean, it WORKED, obviously."

"Yeah, I'm neater than YOU are now," I tell him.

CHECK OUT MY **LOCKER!**

WOW!

"That's unbelievable!" Francis exclaims. "Considering what it USED to look like, it's. . ."

But I've stopped listening. My eyes are locked on a leather case tucked alongside the textbooks on the top shelf.

I examine the case. It's definitely the same camera, right down to the "Property of P.S. 38" tag.

Francis is flabbergasted. "Wha—? How did. . . ? Nate, what's going on?"

"I'll tell you what's going on: NICK thinks he's being FUNNY."

"Nick BLONSKY?" Francis asks in surprise.

"What are you two doing out of class?" He smirks, flashing his hall monitor badge.

"Oh, nothing," I reply angrily.

He shrugs, pretending to be confused. "If I STOLE it, then how can YOU be holding it RIGHT NOW?"

"Because you put it back. During third lesson.

I saw you with it."

Another smirk. "Maybe you did, and maybe you didn't," he says in a singsong voice.

"Because it was HILARIOUS," Nick answers. "That FIGHT you two had when you realised the camera was gone was PRICELESS!"

What a twerp. I'm about two seconds away from

my SECOND fight of the day. "You're a riot," I snarl through gritted teeth.

"We could report you to Principal Nichols for this," Francis adds.

"Dee Dee Holloway, super spy, at your service!" she says, taking a bow.

The tiniest look of uncertainty creeps across Nick's face. "Super spy?"

Dee Dee smiles slyly. "You guys were having such an interesting conversation. . ."

Nick turns pale. He backs away from us, slowly at first. Then he breaks into a run.

I could hug Dee Dee. I don't, of course. But I COULD. "Dee Dee," I tell her gratefully, "that was. . . AWESOME!"

"Yup! The pigeon has landed!" she says, beaming.

Then she grabs me and Francis. "But HERE'S what's REALLY awesome!"

Well, if I didn't hug Dee Dee, I'm sure not going to KISS Francis. I stick out my hand. And so does he, at the exact same moment.

"I shouldn't have accused you of losing the camera," Francis says. "That was lame."

"And I shouldn't have told the whole school your

middle name," I admit. "That was lamer."

"This is FABULOUS!" Dee Dee squeals.

Then, with a gasp, Dee Dee turns me loose. "Nate! There's FOOD on your shirt!"

Makes sense. An hour ago, I was rolling around on the cafetorium floor with Randy. "So?" I ask her.

Suddenly it dawns on me what she's getting at.

Dee Dee's bouncing around like her hair's on fire. "Remember what I said? That a dramatic event might snap you out of it?"

I fling open my locker – my disgustingly neat locker – and grab a pencil and paper.

"If I can draw something without worrying how PERFECT it is, then we'll know I'm not hypnotised any more!"

I go as fast as I can. No rulers. No erasing. And by the time I'm finished, I can tell I'm myself again. Because this definitely isn't perfect.

But it might be the most awesome drawing I've ever made.

11

Nick's not in school the next day. But we don't find
out why until Francis, Teddy, and I walk into the
Chronicle meeting after classes are over.

"Hold it," I say. "Nick gets to stay home from school? For a whole WEEK?"

WHAT A LUCKY STIFF!

That's WAY better than what I got. Principal Nichols gave me three days of detention for fighting with Randy. Then he called my dad. Guess what they talked about?

Why, NO! I DIDN'T hear what happened in the cafetorium!

hairy eyeball

THIS MEETING WILL NOW COME TO ORDER!

BAM BAM BAM BAM BAM BAM BAM

Ugh. Gina and her stinkin' gavel. Couldn't we start the meeting with something a little mellower? Like a foghorn?

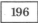

"I've been working on some of these page layouts," Gina announces as we gather around the table. "The group shots look really good. . ."

"What are you trying to PULL, Gina?" Teddy demands angrily. "You only used pictures of YOURSELF and your snobby FRIENDS!"

"And besides, NATE was supposed to supply the candids!" Francis chimes in.

"I'm afraid I can't allow that, Gina," says a voice from behind us.

YES! Hickey to the rescue! Gina turns fire-engine red, then corkscrews her face into a phoney smile.

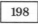

"All right," she says, turning to Francis. "What do YOU want to do?"

Mrs Hickson nods. "I think that's a fair solution. But, Nate, we DO have a deadline, so. . ."

"No problem!" I say immediately. "I should get PLENTY of good candids TOMORROW. . ."

The next morning as we walk to school, I realise two things: (1) it's great to be friends with Francis again, and (2) he's driving me completely insane.

"Nate's right," Teddy says. "You're going to fry your brain before the Trivia Slam even STARTS."

Francis takes a deep breath. "I know, I know."

They COULD. But I still think we'll smuck 'em.

FRANCIS'S FACTOIDS VS. GINA'S (SO-CALLED) GENIUSES

TEAM MEMBER	TRIVIA SPECIALTY	TRIVIA SPECIALTY	TEAM MEMBER
FRANCIS POPE	every-thing	every-thing ...and MORE!	GINA HEMPHILL-TOMS
NATE WRIGHT	comics, Ben Franklin, history of snack foods, Greek myths	science fiction, martial arts, video games	ERIC FLEURY
DEE DEE HOLLOWAY	art, drama, fashion, musical theatre	NO INFO	? ? ? ?
TEDDY ORTIZ	sports, comedy, foreign languages, movie quotes	flute music, cosmetology, reality television	MARY ELLEN POPOWSKI
CHAD APPLEWHITE	breakfast, scouting, lunch, animals, dinner	computer science, math, law enforcement	NICK BLONSKY SUSPENDED

The cafetorium's already mobbed when we get there. "I wonder who Gina will get to replace Nick," Teddy says as we squeeze through the door.

We don't have to wait long to find out.

Wait, did he say "whom"? That's SO Francis. Even when he's trash-talking, he uses good grammar.

Teddy's mouth gapes open. "Is he SERIOUS? Why would Gina put an idiot like RANDY on her team?"

"Randy's no Einstein, but he knows a TON of sports and movie trivia," Francis explains. "Gina's team didn't have anybody like that before."

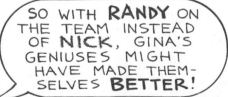

SO WITH **RANDY** ON THE TEAM INSTEAD OF **NICK**, GINA'S GENIUSES MIGHT HAVE MADE THEM- SELVES **BETTER**!

Well. . . MAYBE. But there's no time to worry about it now. Ms Clarke is asking for quiet and explaining the rules.

"You all know the format," she says. "During the preliminary rounds, you may consult your teammates before answering each question. But during the FINAL round. . ."

Shut up? THAT'S the best snappy comeback I've got? Definitely not up to my usual standards. I must be nervous.

"You heard Ms Clarke, Factoids!" Dee Dee says as she reaches into her book bag.

Leave it to Dee Dee to bring costumes into this. But whatever. If wearing dorky hats is going to help us take down Gina's Geniuses, I'm all for it.

"The first question is for Amanda's Pony Posse," Ms Clarke announces.

Pretty easy, right? That's how the Trivia Slam works. The early rounds are ALWAYS a cakewalk. But as the game goes on, the questions get harder.

And the candids get better and better!

Teams start dropping like flies. Tricia's Tater Tots don't know the capital of Luxembourg. (Trick question. It's. . . Luxembourg.) Artur's Antelopes can't name the only vegetable that's also a flower. (Broccoli. Yuck.)

Eventually – just like everyone knew it would – it comes down to two teams.

"OK, guys, here's where all our practising pays off!" Dee Dee whispers. "Try to relax."

RELAX? I can't relax when we're going toe to toe with Gina and Randy. You think they're obnoxious NOW? If they beat us, we'll never hear the end of it.

THE GAME ROLLS ON!

POTASSIUM!	TAXIDERMY.	DENTAL FLOSS.	HAWAII!
JOE.	DARTH VADER!	FIFTY DOLLARS!	A UKULELE?
DAISY DUCK!	P-PURPLE?	A RHOMBUS.	WATER POLO.
THE NILE.	ZERO?	BORSCHT.	UMM...IGOR?

"Nice job, Chad!" I whisper as he steps down from the stage. He looks a little wobbly. The pressure's getting to everybody. And you know what they say about pressure: It breaks stuff. So who's going to crack first?

"Randy," Ms Clarke says, "you're up."

Rats. A sports question. This'll be a no-brainer. Randy grins confidently.

At the beginning of a match, how many pawns are there on a chessboard?

The blood drains from his face. "W-wait a minute. CHESS? Chess isn't a SPORT!"

"It's recognised as a sport by the International Olympic Committee," Ms Clarke states matter-of-factly. "Answer the question, please."

 But Randy's not a chess player. He's more of a tic-tac-toe guy.

Remember, you can't ask your teammates for help in the final round. Randy's got to sink or swim on his own. And I've got a feeling. . .

Ms Clarke shakes her head. "I'm sorry. The answer is sixteen. Eight per side."

Gina looks ready to wring Randy's neck, I'm snapping pictures as fast as I can, and Dee Dee's about to launch into the victory dance she's been rehearsing all week. But it's not over yet.

"If the Factoids answer the next question incorrectly, the game continues," Ms Clarke says. "If they get it right, they're the champions."

I look over at Francis. He flashes me a gigantic smile. Why? Because he knows the same thing I do: We're about to win the Trivia Slam.

"That's correct." Ms Clarke smiles. "Congratu—"

I don't hear the rest. Dee Dee wraps me in a bear hug, and a second later I'm on the bottom of a Factoid pig pile. Teddy's singing in Spanish, hats are flying everywhere. . . it's total pandemonium.

"I thought we were DOOMED when I heard that question!" Chad exclaims as we untangle ourselves.

Before I can answer, Francis slaps me on the shoulder. "He's just really good at trivia, that's all!"

But that's NOT all. And Francis knows it better than anybody.

See, that was my half of the friendship pact I made with Francis back in third grade. He told me his secret – Butthurst – and I told him mine: that I'm a complete cat coward. I know it sounds stupid, but cats just freak me out. They always have.

"Think of it this way," Francis says.

"Ooh! Guys! That reminds me. . ."

As the others scroll through the rest of the pictures, Francis and I step into the hall. "Hey, I just thought of something," he says. "Maybe Uncle Pedro could help you get over your cat phobia."

"No, thanks. Being hypnotised the first time didn't work out so hot."

He chuckles. "Yeah, I'm glad that didn't stick. I like you much better as a slob."

Hear that? Now THAT'S a best friend. We'll always be total opposites, but just because Francis is Mr Clean, it doesn't mean he expects ME to be. He's happy with me just the way I am.